By_____

NO LONGER PROPERTY OF
SEATTLE PUBLIC LIBRARY

Dear Parents:

Congratulations! Your child is taking the first steps on an exciting journey. The destination? Independent reading!

STEP INTO READING® will help your child get there. The program offers five steps to reading success. Each step includes fun stories and colorful art or photographs. In addition to original fiction and books with favorite characters, there are Step into Reading Non-Fiction Readers, Phonics Readers and Boxed Sets, Sticker Readers, and Comic Readers—a complete literacy program with something to interest every child.

Learning to Read, Step by Step!

Ready to Read Preschool–Kindergarten
• big type and easy words • rhyme and rhythm • picture clues
For children who know the alphabet and are eager to begin reading.

Reading with Help Preschool–Grade 1
• basic vocabulary • short sentences • simple stories
For children who recognize familiar words and sound out new words with help.

Reading on Your Own Grades 1–3
• engaging characters • easy-to-follow plots • popular topics
For children who are ready to read on their own.

Reading Paragraphs Grades 2–3
• challenging vocabulary • short paragraphs • exciting stories
For newly independent readers who read simple sentences with confidence.

Ready for Chapters Grades 2–4
• chapters • longer paragraphs • full-color art
For children who want to take the plunge into chapter books but still like colorful pictures.

STEP INTO READING® is designed to give every child a successful reading experience. The grade levels are only guides; children will progress through the steps at their own speed, developing confidence in their reading.

Remember, a lifetime love of reading starts with a single step!

LEGO, the LEGO logo, the Brick and Knob configurations, the Minifigure and NINJAGO
are trademarks and/or copyrights of the LEGO Group.
©2023 The LEGO Group. All rights reserved.

 Manufactured under license granted to AMEET Sp. z o.o.
by the LEGO Group.

AMEET Sp. z o.o.
Nowe Sady 6, 94–102 Łódź—Poland
ameet@ameet.eu
www.ameet.eu

www.LEGO.com

Published in the United States by Random House Children's Books, a division of Penguin Random House
LLC, 1745 Broadway, New York, NY 10019, and in Canada by Penguin Random House Canada Limited,
Toronto.

Step into Reading, Random House, and the Random House colophon are registered trademarks of
Penguin Random House LLC.

Visit us on the Web!
StepIntoReading.com
rhcbooks.com

Educators and librarians, for a variety of teaching tools, visit us at RHTeachersLibrarians.com

ISBN 978-0-593-57096-8 (trade)
ISBN 978-0-593-57097-5 (lib. bdg.)
ISBN 978-0-593-57098-2 (ebook)

Printed in the United States of America
10 9 8 7 6 5 4 3 2 1

Random House Children's Books supports the First Amendment and celebrates the right to read.

3

STEP

READING ON YOUR OWN

STEP INTO READING®

LEGO NINJAGO

LEVEL UP!

based on the story "Sneak Attack!"
by Steve Behling
illustrated by AMEET Studio

Random House 🏠 New York

Kai and his dad, Ray,
had been playing video games
for days.

They were having

a great time!

Kai jumped up
and pumped his fist
in the air when he won
another round.
But Master Wu
was not happy.

Master Wu thought

it was time the two ninja

attended to more important

matters, like Spinjitzu training.

His chicken gave him an idea.

Wu's chicken ran
over to the players.

It even ran across
the game controllers
and wires!
The ninja did not notice.
They were too busy playing.

Then Master Wu tried
turning the temperature
down to make the room
too cold to play in.

Kai noticed the cold—
and so did Wu's chicken!
But Kai did not stop playing.
He used his fire powers
to warm the room.

Cole suggested
that he and Master Wu
leave the house
to attract bad guys.
That would surely get
their attention.
Master Wu decided to try it!

Later that night,
Kai and his dad heard
a noise outside,
but it did not stop them
from playing.

They did not even look up
when Miss Demeanor
and a group of burglars
kicked in the door!

The burglars tore the place apart
looking for the Vengestone.
It was a precious item
that Miss Demeanor wanted.
The burglars made a lot of noise.
They emptied chests
and knocked over bookshelves!

Kai and Ray finally looked up

from their game.

They decided that maybe

they should investigate the noises.

Kai was shocked to find
Miss Demeanor in the hall—
and a burglar eating
his noodles!

Kai and Ray tried to stop
the burglars, but they were
too stiff from sitting
on the couch for so long.

Kai fell over when
one burglar took a vase,
and Ray was too slow
to even land a single punch.

Then Kai surprised
a burglar
by picking him up
and throwing him.
"Power move!" Kai shouted.

Ray cheered.

"It is just like the game!

We need to level up!"

he said.

The burglars surrounded
Kai and Ray.
But the ninja were not
going to back down now.

And they were not
going to let
Miss Demeanor take
the Vengestone!

Miss Demeanor let loose
with a blast from her fire pack.
The ninja acted like they
were in the video game
and leapt over the flames!

Miss Demeanor

and the burglars were shocked.

These ninja had some

nice moves!

Kai and Ray even kicked

Miss Demeanor's

fire pack off her back.

Kai and Ray

continued to level up

to take care of the burglars.

Soon Miss Demeanor
and all the bad guys
were captured.
Master Wu and Cole
were impressed!

Although Kai and Ray
would keep playing
video games, they
promised Master Wu
that they would train
just as much!